THIS BOOK BELONGS TO

children's choice®

BENJY
and his friend
FIFI

for my old Brownie

Benjy and his friend Fifi
Copyright © 1988 by Margaret Bloy Graham
All rights reserved. No part of this book may be
used or reproduced in any manner whatsoever without
written permission except in the case of brief quotations
embodied in critical articles and reviews. Printed in
the United States of America. For information address
Harper & Row Junior Books, 10 East 53rd Street,
New York, N.Y. 10022. Published simultaneously in
Canada by Fitzhenry and Whiteside Limited, Toronto.
10 9 8 7 6 5 4 3 2 1
First Edition

Library of Congress Cataloging-in-Publication Data
Graham, Margaret Bloy.
  Benjy and his friend Fifi / Margaret Bloy Graham.—1st ed.
    p.   cm.
  "A Charlotte Zolotow book."
  Summary: Lovable mutt Benjy accompanies his shy
nervous poodle friend Fifi to her first dog show, where
chaotic adventures ensue.
  ISBN 0-06-022252-2 : $
  ISBN 0-06-022253-0 (lib. bdg.) : $
    [1. Dogs—Fiction. 2. Dog shows—Fiction.] I. Title.
PZ7.G7538Bf 1988   87-29374
[E]—dc19   CIP
                                                      AC

BENJY
and his friend
FIFI

Margaret Bloy Graham

Harper & Row, Publishers   **New York**

Benjy was a brown dog with long ears
and a short tail. He lived with Father,
Mother, Linda, and Jimmy. Benjy loved to play.
Sometimes he played with Jimmy and Linda.

Sometimes he played with Fifi,

who belonged to Mrs. Jones, the lady next door.

Fifi was a shy and nervous poodle,

and Benjy was her only friend.

Tom and Bruno lived down the street.

Whenever they tried to join in the fun,

Fifi ran home. She was scared.

She watched them
from inside the house,
and she felt sad
and lonely.

One day Mrs. Jones rang the bell at Benjy's house.
"I'm putting Fifi in the Dog Show tomorrow,"
she said. "Can Benjy come along
to keep her from getting nervous?"
"Of course," said Mother. "He'd love to."
So the next day
Mrs. Jones and
Fifi called for
Benjy, and off
they went.

The Dog Show was in the park. Dozens and dozens
of dogs were there. Some were being exercised
on the grass, some were being groomed in a big tent,

and some were being judged in a ring.

Benjy wished he could play with them all,

but Fifi wished she could go home. She was scared.

"Here we are," said Mrs. Jones

when they came to the poodle section.

People stared at Benjy.

"That's no poodle," said one. "It's a mutt."

A show judge walked by.

"Only purebreds permitted in the show," he said.

"I'd better hide you, Benjy,"
said Mrs. Jones, and she covered him
with her coat.
Benjy curled up
and went
to sleep.

Mrs. Jones combed and brushed Fifi.
Then she started fixing her topknot.
"Oh dear," she said,
"I forgot the
hair spray.
I'll have
to go back
to the car
and get it."
And she
hurried away.

Fifi was scared again.

She thought she was all alone.

Mrs. Jones had left,

and Fifi couldn't see Benjy.

She tried to follow Mrs. Jones.

She pulled and pulled at her leash,

and twisted and turned

until all of a sudden . . .

she slipped off the table with a yelp!

Benjy woke up.

Where was Fifi?

Then he saw her.

He jumped onto the table

and quickly chewed through the leash.

Fifi dropped to the ground

and raced off in a panic, with Benjy following.

Fifi ran all over the Dog Show, barking and barking.

"Look out for that dog!" shouted someone.

"Don't let it get away!" yelled someone else.

Judges stopped judging, salesmen stopped selling,

photographers stopped taking pictures,

and owners stopped grooming their dogs.

The Dog Show came to a standstill.

Benjy kept following Fifi. It wasn't easy!
They dashed through the hound section.
There was Bruno, and farther on, with
the terriers, Tom. When they saw Benjy,
they pulled away from their owners
and joined in the chase.

After a while Fifi got tired.

She ran behind some boxes and lay down.

Benjy and Bruno and Tom raced past,

and then stopped.

Fifi had disappeared.

Where had she gone?

Tom cocked his head—

he heard a little whine.

Bruno sniffed and sniffed—

he knew Fifi was near.

They went straight to the boxes.

Benjy ran behind the boxes and found Fifi.

She was very, very glad to see him.

Then she saw Bruno and Tom,

and she wasn't scared of them anymore.

Now they were her friends, too.

They'd helped Benjy find her.

Benjy and Fifi ran back to the poodle section.
Fifi led the way.

There was Mrs. Jones. She was crying,
and calling, "Fifi, Fifi, where are you?"

Fifi jumped into Mrs. Jones's arms,

and Benjy ran around them, barking.

"I should never have left you," said Mrs. Jones,

as she hugged and kissed Fifi.

Then she held her at arms' length and stared.

"Fifi," she cried, "you're a mess!

You'll never win a prize now."

But right away she hugged her again and said,

"It doesn't matter.

You're safe

and sound.

We'll try again

next year."

"That brown dog is really clever,"
said another poodle owner. And he told
Mrs. Jones how Benjy had rescued Fifi.
Mrs. Jones hugged
Benjy, too.
"You're a
wonderful friend,"
she said.

"Benjy saved Fifi's life," said Mrs. Jones
when she brought him home. And she told
the family what had happened.
"And guess what," she went on,
"Fifi isn't nervous anymore.
The Dog Show cured her!"

After that, Benjy and Fifi were
better friends than ever.

They had great fun
playing with each other,

and with Bruno and Tom, too.
Mrs. Jones was happy
because Fifi had changed,
and Benjy's family was happy
because *he* hadn't.

The End.